Bost
C

CW00507800

Carol Logan

The Enchanted Violin

THE VIOLIN MADE HER DO IT

Synopsis of the enchanted Violin.

By Carol Logan

A modern Fairy story, set in the city of Cardiff, 'The Enchanted Violin' is a dark mix of reality and fantasy, drawing on the rich mythology of two diverse cultures: China and Wales.

Two Chinese music students, Jay Lee and Xiao Mai, meet at the Welsh School of Music. He is soon obsessed by her, but her love is music. Xiao Mai needs a good instrument to play, otherwise she may be forced to drop out of university, so she sets out with Jay Lee to find one.

One day they hear violin music pouring out from the Castle Arcade, Xiao Mai is overcome and starts to play an imaginary violin on the street. Jay Lee is shocked and forces her to stop. They go together to the Cardiff Violin shop where they meet the Enchanter, an old man dressed in strange clothes from a bygone era, who is not all he seems. He gives Xiao Mai the violin, intending to trap her soul by means of her obsession and imprison it in the instrument.

The Dragon guardians of the city are alerted to the danger by Xiao Mai's, personal zodiac guardian a little wooden dragon door stop. He is joined by a Bengal Tiger Cat, Jay Lee's guardian.

The Enchanter seeks the help of the mythological deities of both cultures, to end Xiao Mai's life. But are thwarted at every turn by the personal guardians of the couple and the dragons, under the command of the Jade Emperor and his son The Great Green Dragon.

At the summer prom Concert, Xiao Mai, watched by Jay Lee and fellow students is performing a solo on top of the castle keep ramparts when the Enchanter seizes his opportunity. Appearing in the guise of a Giant Bird he pushes her to her death. This is the signal for battle to commence between the Dragons and the Enchanters allies.

The Red Dragon General rescues Xia Mai's lifeless body and takes it to the stone circle, leaving her in the care of the guardian he returns to the great battle within the castle walls. A terrible battle between the Green Dragon and the Enchanter ensues and the Green Dragon is impaled on the flag staff, of the castle.

At this juncture The Jade Emperor intervenes, destroying the Enchanter and restoring both his son and Xiao Mai to life. He adopts Xiao Mai and gives her a new name. He rewards Jay Lee by intrusting him with the care of Xiao Mai and gives the couple his blessing.

The Enchanted Violin

Acknowledgements
Photographs by Tony Lloyd
Cover photograph by Tony Lloyd.
Blurb and Preface written by Lynne Barrett Lea
Pencil illustrations by Eric Pilmoor and Carol Logan.
Cover design and Interior by Catherine Murray

The Charity that will benefit in the selling of this book is Pilgrim Hearts. They provide winter night shelter in the local churches and hot meals for the homeless. It is run by Elaine and David Chalmers Brown .

Dedications

To all my students of many cultures and backgrounds, where ever they may be in this world, I dedicate this book to you for you are my inspiration.

Thanks to my teachers at Cardiff University especially Lynn and Bryony you have inspired me and helped more than you will ever know.

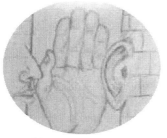

Chapter 1

The Beginning

All cities have secrets. Secret places, hidden paths, court-yards, gardens. Stories never told but known, oh yes they are known, deep dark deeds committed . . . but never talked about. But the walls and monuments of the cities know. They know everything, for they are the silent witnesses to all that goes on within the city.

The walls, and especially the Dragon monuments of Cardiff, the beautiful little capital city of Wales, know everything there is to know about the city and its secrets. They know the hidden places just off the wide, tree-lined avenues with tiny paths leading somewhere. They know the places in the main streets between two forbidding-looking houses, where you may stumble upon a secret passage or two that lead to hidden courtyards and arcades. They know that in the Castles, (for Cardiff has two, not ruins you understand but vibrant, alive Castles, one in the centre and one on the outskirts of the city, guarding the pass leading to the heartland of Wales) the castle walls hold within their very stones records of blood-thirsty secrets of murder and intrigue. The walls also know that in the secret alleys and behind front doors, in the pubs and cafes, inside the famous University and in the student halls and houses, lurk secrets, old secrets and new secrets. The very fabric of Cardiff is steeped in secrets, some to be told and others never ever to be revealed.

Then in the great parks that sweep outwards from the city centre, the trees are privy to secrets and as they dip their toes into the rushing river Taff, or the lake in Roath Park, they learn from the water, secrets of the past and the now. They know the tales of the ancient Kings of Wales, Uther Pen Dragon, Arthur Pen Dragon, the great wizard Merlin and the evil Morgana Le Fay. They know that often strange things occur in the park after the ordinary person has gone home. They see the animals from the Castle's magical Animal Wall, slip off the wall just as the great clock strikes twelve midnight, and catch them prowling through the park or slaking their thirst at the Taff's brink. The trees are party to the other dimension, the one not seen by the human eye or touched by the human heart.

They witness the Dragon Guardians gather for their nightly debrief on the ramparts of the Castle. Dragons are everywhere guarding this city, proud to be the symbol of Wales. They have watched over this land of mountains, sea, waterfalls, mists and song since the dawn of time, protecting it from invaders.

Until in recent years there came an invasion that needed no army to stem its flow. A peaceful invasion from another Dragon-loving country thousands of miles away on the other side of the world; a country equally steeped in mystery, legends and song. A country where its people are fiercely proud of their heritage and learning; a country that sends its finest students to study at Cardiff University. The great country of China, where so many ancient symbols and beliefs are similar, but not quite the same, as the Welsh. So let us begin at the beginning.

There is a tale to tell and the telling of it is long and in places painful. It is a tale of two cultures, each hold Dragons in high esteem and regard them as protectors; it involves the animals of the Chinese (zodiac) and deities of mythology as well as the ancient Celtic Guardians of Wales, who step out of the mists of time to once again play a part in this story. The tale needs to be told and others need to learn from its telling. It begins in the past, not the distant past you understand, like most fairy stories, where truth is hidden within fantasy, but in the very real present past, in this very city of Cardiff, in this very place. And so begins my tale.

Xiao Mai, an eighteen-year-old first-year music major student, was given a part-scholarship by the government of China to study music at Cardiff University. Xiao Mai came from a very poor family in the province of Gansu, China, and the whole of her village had saved hard so that they could help fund her tuition fees. The only thing she had to find was money to live on and money for a really good violin. Her teachers at the University said hers was not a very good one.

'You need an instrument with a voice,' they said. 'Yours just isn't good enough.'

'Something like a Stradivarius, a Maggini or a modern Daniel Burgess,' they suggested.

'Any of those would be worthy of your talent,' they flattered. Each teacher themselves was eager to hold and experience the thrill of playing an instrument made by one of the world's ancient master violin makers.

Xiao Mai was very sad. She had no idea how to get the money for the violin or for food to live on. She only had one pound a day to buy food with, all the rest of her small income went on rent, bills and music. She had no idea how she could get enough money to live on, let alone buy a new violin. If she had a good instrument perhaps she could busk in the streets around Cardiff Castle. She had seen many young people playing guitars around there; people threw money into their instrument cases. Perhaps she could even sacrifice a pound or two, maybe even three, go to London on the Mega Bus and play in Covent Garden Market. The tourists there were very generous to musicians who played in the below ground-level courtyards; most were students at the London Guild Hall School of Music. Perhaps she could join them, or get a group from Cardiff to go with her. Perhaps her fellow musician house-mates at number 12 Fanny Street, or her best friend at University, a fellow Chinese called Jay Lee Woo, would go with her.

She liked Jay Lee, not because he came from a very wealthy family in Beijing and owned a Daniel Burgess violin, as well as a cello that had once been played by the great cellist Jacqueline Du Pré, but because he was kind to her and made her laugh. She knew that if they were both studying at Xian University School of Music, Jay Lee would know his place and not be as friendly with a girl from such a poor background as hers. Perhaps she might be able to persuade Jay Lee to play duets with her and they could earn money together, she on the violin and he on the wonderful cello. Jay Lee once told her that he was sure he could still hear the cello playing 'The Swan' from Saint-Saens 'Carnival of Animals' the very way Jacqueline used to play it.

'Perhaps her spirit is in the cello,' he joked.

'Don't joke about such things,' Xiao Mai scolded him 'as a good communist, you are not supposed to believe in such things.'

But Jay Lee just laughed.

Xiao Mai longed to have a violin every bit as good as the cello Jay Lee played. Sometimes she would play his violin and it was lovely, but she longed for one of her own, preferably an old one.

'Wouldn't it be wonderful', she thought 'if I could find a violin like the one Yehudi Menuhin used to play, perhaps I can discover one in a junk shop, car boot or on E-Bay'. Xiao Mai knew that here in Britain people discovered treasures all the time hidden away in dusty attics, dry cellars and secret places. She had seen miracles like that happen, when she had watched Bargain Hunt and the Antiques Road Show on Jay Lee's portable television. All she had to do was keep looking.

It was a Saturday morning in late October, Jay Lee and Xiao Mai were walking along the road past the University buildings, kicking up the autumn leaves as they went. The air was chill and there was a hint of fog. As they reached the Bute Building, Jay Lee pointed to the entrance where a large snarling Red Dragon, wings uplifted, right front leg held high, holding a red circlet of laurel leaves in his sharp red claws, stood on guard.

'See Xiao Mai,' he said softly 'see, there is one of the

Jade Emperor's Dragon Generals.'

She looked up and encountered the eye of the creature, which seemed to be looking straight at her. She could have sworn that the eye blinked.

'As we go past the University Registration Building you will see more Little Dragons on the railings,' Jay Lee laughed teasingly, 'as you pass by they will salute you.'

Xiao Mai looked, but rather than saluting her they seemed to hide or turn away their little heads.

'Look up there,' Jay Lee pointed to the great dome over the City Council building. 'See the Chief Dragon General.'

She looked; sure enough, coiled on top of the huge dome was a great green Dragon that had once been a shining bronze Dragon.

'He is the son of the Jade Emperor!'

Xiao Mai did not comment, but looked again at the Green General with more interest. She knew from tales her grandmother had told her that the Jade Emperor was the chief deity in heaven. Once, in the old days before the Second World War and the revolution when the communists had taken charge, the whole of China had believed in the Jade Emperor and his stories were told and passed down by the story-tellers and keepers of the traditions, the old people of the countryside. These old keepers of the stories still told the tales but in the oral telling of them how much had been added or how much had been lost over the years and centuries nobody knew. But there was always a kernel of truth in a legend or so she had been told wasn't there?

Grandma had said that The Emperor was originally the Crown Prince of the kingdom of 'Pure Felicity and

Majestic Heavenly Lights and Ornaments.' Grandmother had told her that at his birth an amazing bright light had shone from him that filled every corner of the kingdom of China. And while he was growing up he was very clever and very kind and very wise. Throughout his childhood he had been the champion of the poor and needy people. Eventually he had become the King of Heaven. How she wanted to be like the Jade Emperor, kind to all creatures (man and beast) clever and wise. How she longed for fame and fortune. She wanted to help Grandma, give her a comfortable life in her old age. She wanted to be able to provide electricity and running water to the villagers who had sacrificed for her. She wanted so much to give each and every one a decent place to live and a better life. She knew that the only way she could achieve both was to work very hard and be completely devoted to her studies. She did not really have time to have a nan paniol (boyfriend) and she was pretty sure that was what Jay Lee wanted her to be. His girlfriend. She glanced sideways at him as they walked along the street. He did not attempt to hold her hand, but every so often his hand brushed hers and she snatched it away immediately. When it came to crossing the street his hand grabbed her elbow to make sure she crossed safely, but then once over, it dropped to his side again and he continued to chat animatedly.

'There are Dragons everywhere in Cardiff,' went on Jay Lee, 'they are silent and they watch. They watch over us Chinese students, like Guardians.'

Xiao Mai arched her eyebrow, a questioning gesture.

'How?' she said quietly, 'Do the dragons of Cardiff guard us Chinese students? They are just statues."

'If we are in trouble they will come to our rescue.'

Xiao Mai smiled. Jay Lee was a great story-teller. She liked his fantasy about the Dragons being the special Guardians of the Chinese students but she did wonder just how the dragons would come to their rescue if they needed it. But here in this city, this beautiful little capital city of Wales, they did not need guardians they had freedom to pursue their dreams, the city was safe, what could threaten them here? But she decided that Jay Lee was too good a friend to argue with especially over his little fantasy about the dragon guardians.

'Let's go to the Castle,' she said cheerfully. 'Perhaps we will find more of your Dragon Guardians there.'

They turned right at the end of the road, instead of straight ahead under the road to go to town, and ambled towards Bute Park. The day was young, they were young and they had all the time in the world. They entered the park through the small gateway beside the large modern boat-like Music and Drama building of the University and walked through the park, past the ring of grey granite standing stones, out through the entrance by the gatehouse Tea Room, and along the Animal Wall by the Castle.

'Do these Guardians come alive as well?' She asked.

'If the Green General needs their services,' he replied.

She laughed a merry little laugh; Jay Lee loved to hear her laugh.

Coming to the Castle entrance, they crossed the road by the zebra-crossing opposite the Welsh Souvenir shop, where Bob the ex-policeman presided over hand-carved love spoons.

'If I were to have a love spoon carved for you,' Jay Lee said softly 'It would have to have a violin somewhere in the design.'

Xiao Mai smiled and wondered if he ever would buy her a love spoon or give her a Jade bracelet, which was the ancient symbol of engagement and marriage in China.

'And a Dragon,' she said softly, 'I was born in the year of the Dragon.'

'Were you? I was born in the year of the Tiger,' he replied.

'Then you would have to have a cello, a violin and a tiger on your love spoon', she teased. Then a look full of longing came into her eyes.

'What is it? What are you thinking about? I know you well enough now to know that there is something you are not telling me…Come on Xiao Mai I am your friend you can tell me.' He pleaded.

Xiao Mai hesitated she was a private person and did not often reveal her true innermost thoughts and feeling to even her closest friends and certainly not to her parents. On the other hand she did reveal them to Grandma, she was a good keeper of secrets and she had so much wisdom. How Xiao Mai missed sharing things with her grandmother.

She took in a sharp inhalation of the fresh air, how clean and pure the air in this city was in comparison to the heavily polluted air of her own nearest city. Her thoughts ran on should she? Shouldn't she confide in Jay Lee? She let her breath out slowly and decided she knew enough about him to trust him.'

'What I would like, more than anything,' she said wistfully, 'is a really good violin.'

Chapter 2

The Music Shop

They were hovering outside the Welsh shop, looking at the beautifully carved wooden love spoons, when they heard music coming from the old Victorian arcade, just a few metres down the road. A sign above the entrance proclaimed it as the Castle Arcade. The music curled out from between the two coffee shops either side of the arcade and danced its way towards them. Xiao Mai was transfixed, rooted to the spot, her almond eyes fixed on a distant place within her body. Her stance changed mechanically to that of a musician holding a violin and the fingers of her left hand moved up and down the invisible finger- board in perfect synchronisation with the notes that drifted out from between the two shops. Her right hand held an invisible bow; passion was in her playing as the beautiful strains of 'The Fire and Blood' violin concerto by Michael Dougherty poured forth, note upon glorious note, from the invisible violin.

Jay Lee was alarmed, he took her hand, stopped her in mid-bow. Her fingers continued to play the notes on the invisible finger-board.

'Soba nu paniol,' (come girlfriend) he said softly. She did not move, but her fingers stopped hitting the invisible strings. Again he said 'Women soba Nu paniol. Women tu Shandian ma?' (Let's go girlfriend. Shall we go to the shops?)

At the sound of her native mandarin, Xiao Mai's eyelids fluttered and she walked hand in hand with Jay Lee into the arcade.

They walked the length of the arcade, past the vineyard shop with its green and gold lettering and an enticing display of wine, past the shop that sold dear little handmade shoes for children, and on to the cheese shop at the end where they turned sharp left and walked past the two cafés on the left and right. Just by the stone steps leading to the upper gallery, they found a fourteen-inch white viola in a glass case. It had obviously been painted, no self-respecting viola would want to be that colour.

The music continued to spill down the stairs, enticing them to the upper gallery shops. They crossed the iron bridge with its red and white wrought-iron sides and jumped down the four steps to the row of shops that proclaimed Cardiff Violins, Makers and Repairers. A notice in one of the windows gave the information that violins were bought, sold, repaired and made by the proprietor of the shop. A red arrow pointed them to the last shop and, there in the window, they saw it; a beautiful violin resting in a battered brown crocodile-skin case, lying at the spike of a majestic double bass. Tiny sparks of light darted from the pegs holding the strings, whilst the strings themselves were vibrating as if an unseen bow was being drawn over them with passion. As they looked they could see the strings shortening and lengthening as unseen fingers came down on the finger-board. Music poured forth from the instrument, creeping under the door and escaping into the arcade. Everyone else seemed oblivious to the music. It was as if they were all suddenly stone deaf. Xiao Mai was entranced.

'Let's go in,' she said.

As they pushed open the door of the old music shop the wonderful music ceased and the strings were silent; the music died. An ancient brass bell tinkled in the far reaches of the dusty shop. Eventually, after what seemed an age, an ancient thin-looking man appeared in a scruffy, blue, white and purple patchwork Jalapa, like those worn by the Jedi in star wars. On his head of long, sparse, grey-white hair, he wore a gold embroidered round cap with a long golden tassel to one side. On his feet were black and gold embroidered slippers with curly toes. His moustache and beard were like those of the ancient sages on the wall paintings of famous Grottoes near Dunhuang in northern Gansu.

'Can I help you?' His voice was mellow, like a cello.

'Please,' said Xiao Mai 'please can we look at the violin in the window? Can we play it?'

The old man looked them up and down with piercing black eyes like ripe blackberries.

'Can you play?'

'Oh yes!' they both exclaimed, 'We can play.'

'We are music majors at the University!' exclaimed Jay Lee importantly, puffing out his chest with pride. 'I own a David Burgess violin.'

The old man's eyes softened, 'Ah, a Burgess,' he said softly, 'you must be very rich to own one of them. A beautiful instrument . . . very beautiful, with such a lovely voice . . . such a lovely voice . . . 'His voice drifted into a whisper.

The old man reached into the window and brought out the ancient battered crocodile-leather case with its contents.

'Not the original case,' he observed cryptically, handing the case and its contents to Jay Lee. 'The last owner, or so I am led to believe, was given the case as a gift by a rich Egyptian. Its real Nile crocodile-skin and, as such, is the Guardian of the violin.' His voice purred, reminding Jay Lee of a contented cat.

Jay Lee took the instrument and examined it very carefully. He turned it over and looked at its back, wood like a tiger-skin; he felt excitement rise up inside him as he stroked the smooth contours and surface. The man laughed.

'It isn't a Strad,' he said, 'everyone hopes they will find a Strad, but this one isn't the right colour.'

'What do you mean?' Jay Lee lovingly cradled the instrument.

The old man's voice dropped to a conspiratorial whisper, 'I have been told the ancient master violin-makers used human blood in the varnish.'

The strings of the violin quivered and a thin e-string voice whispered, 'Play me, oh please play me.'

'Some say it is not human blood but Dragon's blood' he went on, his eyes fixed on Xiao Mai as if he were trying to read her soul. 'Not real Dragon's blood, you understand, but the juice of Dragon berries. It's the varnish that makes the violin produce such a wonderful sound.' The man chuckled and shrugged his bony shoulders, 'but there are many theories.'

'Didn't tell us about the blood at Uni did they Xiao Mai?'

She shook her head.

Jay Lee tipped the instrument and peered inside the sound box.

'It does say Antonio Stradivarius, Cremona 1718 on the label . . . right in the middle of his golden period,' he said thoughtfully 'and the back does have the distinctive tiger markings to the wood. The pegs are ebony, each with tiny diamond fragments set in gold.'

His words hung between them like an icy barrier.

'Perhaps the violin was made by an apprentice of Stradivarius . . . There are many fakes, many copies.' The man shrugged his shoulders and sucked at his thin whiskers. 'Now a true Stradivarius, it is said, needs to have virgin's blood in the final coat of varnish . . . but who knows what the master used, he carried his secret to the grave.'

'My back is red,' sang the voice. 'Red . . . red, painted with the blood of young girls who have never been wed.'

Xiao Mai shuddered slightly, *'instruments don't talk,' she said to herself, 'I really must stop listening to Jay Lee's stories'.* But already she was under the spell of the instrument.

'Play me Xiao Mai . . . I will sing to you. I will tell you secrets . . . I will give you your heart's desire . . .'

'Want to play it little lady?'

'Can I?'

The old man nodded, handing Jay Lee the bow.

Jay lee reluctantly handed Xiao Mai the violin, picked

up the bow, tightened it and started to rosin the white horse hair. As Xiao Mai tightened the strings of the instrument the little diamonds sparkled enticingly, the violin seemed to be flirting with her . . . it giggled in a little e-string voice.'

'So nice to be in the arms of a girl . . . girls are gentle, they know how to treat things well. Boys are heavy handed; they do not get the best from me . . .'

Xiao Mai started in surprise. This time she really had heard a voice.

'Did you hear that voice?'

'What voice?' asked Jay Lee, busily rosining the bow to a powdery white.

The old man's eyes crinkled and hardened and a secret smile played over his thin lips.

'Play me . . .' the e-string voice said again . . . 'play me and you will discover something.'

Xiao Mai reached for the bow. She tucked the violin in between her left shoulder and chin, resting her chin on the black chinrest. Holding the bow in her right hand, small finger spread out along its shank, she brought the bow down on the strings and started to play scales.

'I hate scales' sang the violin. 'Play something else, let us sing together.'

As Xiao Mai drew the bow softly across the strings, the violin's pure voice rose, whirling, swirling around the shop, into the arcade, spilling out onto Castle Street in an emotional rendering of Handel's Largo.

'What fun!' sang the violin. 'What fun! You play well, Xiao Mai . . . You play so well.'

Xiao Mai's fingers flew up and down the finger-board.

'Buy me. Buy me Xiao Mai and I will tell you dark,

deep, secrets . . . you will play in the greatest concert halls of the world if you buy me. I will play my heart out for you . . . the world will be at your feet . . . I will be your slave until . . . '

Xiao Mai smiled; she had released the spirit of the violin. As she played and listened to the enticing voice, an overwhelming desire to own the instrument came upon her.

'Be careful. Oh, be careful what you wish for and what you do,' whispered a voice. It seemed to come from a little wooden red Welsh Dragon that was acting as a door stop . . . but Xiao Mai did not listen; she was transfixed.

Jay Lee saw the enraptured look on her face.

'How much does it cost?' He asked. 'How much do you want for the old violin?'

'To own an instrument like this demands great sacrifice on the part of the owner,' said the old man softly, 'to play it takes the love of a pure young girl . . . the violin needs that in order to sing like an angel. That love must be devoted to the violin alone. It chooses its own owner and it seems to have chosen your girlfriend. In order for her to own and play the instrument, you must sacrifice your love for her because she will become possessed by the instrument. She will soar to great heights . . . she will forget about you . . . but then . . .' he shook his head. But then . . .'

'But then . . . WHAT?' demanded Jay Lee, raising his voice...

'She will die unless you discover someone to pay the ultimate sacrifice for her. Only the Jade Emperor knows what that sacrifice will be . . .'

'What do you know about the Jade Emperor?'

demanded Jay Lee.

'Ah, he is in the past history of your country,' said the old man. 'Once you believed in him and in the Dragon Guardians but he, and they, have been banished by communism for many years now. You Chinese believe in nothing. All the old stories and beliefs are gone. Lost . . . What a pity . . . What a pity . . .' the old man shook his head in mock sorrow. 'You are at the mercy of everything that is evil in mankind because you have no belief in the Ying and the Yang, the good and the bad.'

'Who are you?' Jay Lee felt a tug of fear deep inside his heart.

'Ah,' said the old man 'Who am I? Well my son, I belong to the old times that is all you need to know. I belong to the old times, but for something I did, I have to live on . . . and on . . . and on, creating more violins . . . until the Jade Emperor passes judgement.'

'Oh dear, oh dear,' exclaimed the Little Dragon 'I am not doing my job of Guardian very well. The evil Enchanter is at his evil work again, seducing the young and vulnerable.' The Little Dragon wrung his claws in distress. 'What will the Great Green Dragon say about this? The enchantment is too great. I fear for this girl's life.'

'You must stop her playing!' yelled Jay Lee, frantic with worry. 'She cannot, she must not have this instrument. I will give her my David Burgess! Stop her! Please stop her!'

'Even if I stop her, and believe me I can stop her physically playing it, but I cannot stop her longing for it. You see she and it are one now, like in a marriage. It has her soul in its grasp. Nothing else, no one else, matters for her now. She does not need you Jay Lee! Now she has the violin, SHE DOES NOT NEED YOU.' The Enchanters voice had risen gradually to a crescendo.

'Oh dear! Oh dear!' exclaimed the Little Dragon in his reedy voice, worriedly flapping his tiny red wings. 'The Great Green Dragon General will court-martial me for this, sleeping whilst on guardian duty and failing to act when danger threatened. Oh dear what am I to do?'

Jay Lee took a deep breath, and in his sternest voice said very firmly:

'Xiao Mai, Soba!' (Let's Go)

She ignored him and carried on playing.

Jay Lee grasped her right hand which was plying the bow, the violin made a screeching protest as the bow slid over the strings towards the lower reaches of the finger-board. Jay Lee prised her fingers open one by one, until he had the bow in his grasp. All the time the fingers of her left hand were positioning themselves on the finger-board, and the instrument kept letting out little plinks as its strings lengthened and shortened under Xiao Mai's flying fingers. Next he gently prised the violin from her and quickly locked it in the battered old case, along with the bow.   The case shut with a snap, like the mouth of a crocodile snapping its teeth together onto its unsuspecting prey.

Taking Xiao Mai by the shoulders, he shook her fiercely.

'Wake up Xiao Mai, wake up! You are under a spell! Wake up!'

He snapped his fingers in front of her eyes. But still they stared fixedly ahead. He turned to the old man.

'Do something,' he pleaded, 'it is your violin, you enticed her to play it, you drew her here with the music.

Please . . . please bring her back to normal.'

'Ahhh,' the old man let out a long sigh. 'But you did not stop her did you? You had the power to stop her. You recognised the danger, I saw it in your eyes, but you did not stop her. Now you will have to live with the consequences of your neglect. Unless the Jade Emperor intervenes, this girl will never be normal again. There will be times when she will seem normal, but from now on, she will only live for music and will be in the controlling power of the violin and of me.' He folded his hands firmly into the sleeves of his Jalapa.

Jay Lee flashed him a glance of utter loathing, wishing he had never set eyes on this odious man.

'Come nu paniol, (Girlfriend) come,'

'She can't hear you,' whispered the Little Dragon, she can't hear you Jay Lee Woo, and you can't hear me. If only I could talk into your mind, but then I am not your Guardian, I am Xiao Mai's . . . Oh dear, Oh dear. What a mess! What a mess!'

'Come Xiao Mai,' Jay lee spoke softly, as if to a sleepwalking child. Come I will take you home . . . '

'Then you will have to take the violin as well,' said the old man calmly, 'because she has just hired it with her soul. She was tempted and she fell for that temptation. Eventually, she will pay for that temptation with her life.'

Jay Lee stared at him in horror, not believing the words he had just heard fall from the old man's thin lips. Xiao Mai was trapped, he was trapped. In a strange city . . . in a foreign country. What on earth were they to do?

Chapter 3

The Guardians

Xiao Mai's eyes flicked open, but she stared straight ahead, locked in her own little world. She bent down and lifted the battered old crocodile-skin violin case into her arms and cradled it to her breast. Slowly she walked out of the door, turned right, climbed the four steps to the bridge, and crossed it; she did not notice her reflection in the huge glass mirrors either end of the arcade, her eyes were fixed, she walked like a zombie. Looking neither to the right nor to the left, she descended the four steps on the other side of the bridge, then turned, descended the sixteen stone steps, and out into the arcade. At the foot of the stairs she turned left onto the slate-grey tiles of the floor of the arcade and past the café tables with cheerful little candles burning in jam jars on their surfaces. A few customers, wrapped in cosy lap blankets, sipping coffee, stopped, cups poised mid-air, as they stared after the pretty Chinese girl.

On she went, past the fine arts shop with its beautiful

paintings and prints until she came to Claire Rangers Jewellery shop at the very entrance to the arcade. There she turned left towards the Castle, and, like a mechanical doll, walked into St Mary's street and towards the Goat Major pub at the end of the road. She did not run, she did not speak, and without waiting for the light to turn green on the pedestrian crossing, she marched across the road looking neither to the right nor to the left of her. Cars screeched to a stop, missing each other by a whisker. The driver of the red open-top Cardiff Tour bus shook his fist at her.

'Look where you are going! Bloody foreigner!' he yelled. 'You need to learn how to cross roads young lady. You are not in Beijing now!'

Xiao Mai just kept on walking, completely oblivious to the fracas she had just caused.

'*She is going into the Castle,*' thought Jay Lee, '*She doesn't have the Castle keys pass so she won't be able to get in*'. He watched from the shadow of the souvenir shop as Xiao Mai turned left again and walked along by the Castle walls until she reached the Animal Wall. As if touched by a magic wand, all the creatures shuffled uneasily and their heads turned with alarm in their eyes as she passed by, with the crocodile-skin case still clasped tightly to her chest. Close at her heels, like a little Skye terrier, half running, half flying, came the little Red Dragon.

'Danger! Danger! Danger!' he called in his high little voice. The watching animals on the wall heard him, but the passers-by didn't.' One of you get a message to the Dragon Generals,' he shrieked 'Tell them that the Nile Crocodile is loose, tell them that an innocent girl has been deceived into playing the forbidden violin . . . tell them that she is in danger of losing her soul . . . tell them, tell them.'

Just then the Westminster chimes rang out from the great clock tower, followed by three great booms telling the hour. Then another half boom, just as the last sound vibrated into oblivion. Xiao Mai reached the Tea House by the gate of Bute Park. She woke up from her trance and looked around her. *How had she got here? What was this old violin case doing in her arms?* She remembered nothing, nothing at all about the shop, the man in the blue patchwork Jalapa, or anything else that had happened that morning. *But where was Jay Lee?* She turned and looked back towards the Castle and saw Jay Lee running along by the Animal Wall, waving and calling to her.

'Xiao Mai WAIT . . . FOR . . . ME...E...EE!'

Neither of them saw the little Red Dragon watching them from under the late-blooming red geraniums in the green window box on the Tea Room windowsill.

'Why did you just walk out of the shop like that?' he demanded. 'You stole that violin!'

Xiao Mai looked at Jay Lee in amazement.

'Stole the Violin? Me? What on earth do you mean?'

'You just picked up the case, clasped it to your heart and walked out.'

'Really?'

'Yes really! Just as well the old man, the shop keeper, was so impressed by your playing he said you could borrow the violin until your Uni course was over, on one condition: that you go and play for him once a month.'

'Did he? How wonderful, how kind of him!' As Xiao Mai hugged the violin case in delight, she heard a tinkling little chuckle from inside the case . . .

'Oh dear,' sighed the little Red Dragon letting out a breath. 'That evil old Enchanter, the keeper of the violins' souls, has put his spell on Jay Lee as well. He does not remember what has happened or what was said to him by the Enchanter, or what he said back to him, or the fact that he very nearly hit the Enchanter in his rage. All has been wiped clean from his memory. Poor Jay Lee, he is about as useful in a situation like this as a flea. He is supposed to be the strong one in the relationship. The boy is supposed to look after the girl, that is what the Jade Emperor intended in the beginning, but once again the male of the species has let our Lord and Master down.'

The Little Dragon sighed again, this time a deep, sad, frustrated sigh. Just then he saw a Bengal Tiger cat stalk through the gate of the park and start to rub its body against Jay Lee's legs, all the while fixing his eyes on the Little Dragon. Thoughts passed between them. Thoughts that manifested in unspoken words; each could read the other's mind. The spoken word is not need by those in tune with one another.

'Thank goodness you have come' thought the little Red Dragon. 'I presume you are Jay Lee's Guardian?'

'I am indeed,' purred the cat, directing his unspoken words into the mind of the Dragon. 'Not as big as I should be, but then this is Wales, we cannot scare the locals. If I were to assume my true size there would be police and vets everywhere and I would end up in Bristol Zoo tranquilised. That is why when Jay Lee came to Wales the Jade Emperor down-sized me. But I am just as effective, my scaly Little Dragon friend.'

The Little Dragon snorted and a little puff of smoke escaped from his nostrils.

'*I presume,*' the cat continued, directing his stream of thoughts into the mind of the Dragon, '*I presume that you are the girl's Guardian?*'

The Dragon nodded.

'*And this thing,*' he waved a paw in the direction of the violin case, ''*this crocodile thing is what we have to protect these two humans from?*'

The Dragon nodded again.

'*We have to protect them from what is inside.*'

'*Well what is inside?*'

'*The . . . forbidden . . . instrument!*'

The cat's eyes narrowed. '*Do these two know the danger they are in? Have they seen the wicked Enchanter, the keeper of the souls of all who play the instrument of death?*'

The Dragon nodded and blew his thoughts towards the cat. '*I need to report to the Generals, there is great danger afoot. The evil Enchanter, keeper of the forbidden instrument, is once again on the loose, seeking the souls of young women through their obsession with that violin and fame.*'

'*I will guard these two, persuade them to have a cup of tea,*' the message flashed through golden eyes, '*you go and report and get back here quickly . . . I presume they are safe as long as she does not open the case?*'

'*Quite right,*' thought-responded the Dragon. '*Quite right, as long as she does not open that case and play the violin, you are safe. If she does, then she cannot be released until the City Clock chimes the unusual hour.*'

The Little Dragon spread his tiny red wings and, like a red autumn leaf, he danced upwards catching a thermal. He sailed away towards the great dome where the Great Green Dragon sat watching and guarding the city.

𝕮hapter 4

Within the Stone Circle.

As she climbed the night sky the Moon Princess shone her silvery light down upon Bute Park and the great sombre circle of twelve standing stones, lighting and making stark contrast of the depths of shadows amongst the hibernating trees. Shards of silver highlighted the edges of branches, delicate as French lace. The great dark grey stones stood like sentinels around the central altar-stone, waiting.

Like a tiny helicopter, a double sycamore seed wing launched itself from the top twig of the nearest sycamore tree and whirled downwards, landing gently amid the hoar-encrusted silver grass. From it stepped a tiny figure no bigger than the smallest ladybird, but perfect in every detail. It was the Enchanter, dressed in his strange clothes but this time with a silver coolie hat on his head and his long, grey-white hair scraped back from his face into a long rope-like pig tail which hung down his back. As he stood there he began to grow larger and larger and larger

. . . until he towered over the largest stone. He stood silently waiting, his face in shadow, and his arms hidden in the sleeves of his Jalapa.

There was a stirring behind the old lime tree and out from the shadows stepped Ankou (an ancient Celtic deity), the collector of dead souls. She was tall and haggard, dressed in long robes of white and grey. Her long, grey-white hair with a streak of burgundy flowed around her skeletal face and over her bony shoulders. She stepped into the ring of stones and bowed to the Enchanter, then without a word walked silently to the stone next to him and took her place. Next to join the circle was Jui Wei Hu, a nine-tailed fox from China; he slunk to his position without as much as a whisker turning in the direction of the Enchanter. Then the sound of distant hooves was heard coming from the direction of the river Taff and there, beautiful in the moonlight, stood Ceffyl-Dwr, the Water Horse whose very beauty denied the evil that she was capable of wreaking upon the unsuspecting traveller.

Soon the Three Keepers of Hell emerged out of the darkness of the surrounding rhododendron bushes. Ma Micu, a powerful horse, responsible for catching the souls of sinners before they escaped justice, Mu Tu, whose job it was to use his ox-like strength to make sure that prisoners did not escape from hell, and finally Pun Guan, The Lord of Hell, who assigned souls to their own private hell. Silently each took his place in the circle beside a great stone, until all twelve were occupied by some evil or other from the lands of Chinese and Welsh mythology.

The Enchanter's blackberry-dark eyes swept around

the stone circle, resting briefly on each of the creatures in turn, as he silently acknowledged their presence. A thin smile of satisfaction curled around his lips as all kow-towed, bending from the waist as the Enchanter's gaze rested on them. They did not notice that high in the lime tree above their heads an owl was sitting, watching, waiting and listening.

The Enchanter stepped forward to the centre of the stone circle, to the altar stone itself, where dry branches lay as if ready for a bonfire. Bending over, he selected the largest branch, the king of all branches, and drove its sharp, jagged end into the soft earth. He then reached into the capacious pockets of his Jalapa and withdrew a large box of extra-long Cameo matches, (manufactured in China). Slowly he opened the box and extracted a long white match with fluorescent pink tip. He struck the match sharply against the side of the box. The flame flared as match hit box. He reached out and ignited the dry leaves on the end of his branch. Then he stood silently, glowering from under bushy eyebrows, as the

Creatures of Evil, each in turn, stepped forward, selected a branch, and lit it from the one he now held in his left hand. The flames flared and glowed. Then each returned to his allotted place in the great stone circle. Each rammed the flaming torch into the soft earth.

From where the owl sat in the great tree he could see a perfect circle of fire. Each face illuminated, not kindly faces, but faces bent on evil mischief, bent and twisted with evil thoughts. Faces marked by dastardly deeds that lurked deep in their souls. There was no inner light or radiance and calm. There was no beauty reflected in those faces gathered there. It is said that true beauty comes from a lovely soul. Those gathered at the stone circle had turned their backs on the giver of love and beauty. They had rejected the Jade Emperor, turned their backs on his offer of a home in his beautiful kingdom and chosen instead to serve the wicked Enchanter.

'I have summoned you together tonight,' the Enchanter's voice was mellow like the Cello in his shop window, 'for a very important meeting.' He paused, sucking in his long drooping whiskers.

'The enchanted violin is about to claim another soul.' He paused for effect. But there was not a sound, not even a sigh; all the eyes of evil were fixed on his face.

'So the violin has not yet claimed her soul?' The icy voice belonged to Ankou.

The Enchanter shook his head.

'So what is the problem . . . is the girl not obsessed by the violin . . . has not the Crocodile of the Nile, the Guardian of the violin, done his duty and made sure that she thinks of nothing else but the violin?' Her voice was cold and harsh and cut like the icicles that were beginning to form on the trees.

The Enchanter shook his head 'She has an admirer, a best friend . . . someone who would like to make her more than just a friend.'

'Then we have a problem,' bellowed Mu Tu.

'A bigger problem than you think,' retorted the Enchanter. 'He is Chinese as well. And he is prepared to die for her rather than let her die.'

'Bit late for that now,' remarked Pu Guan, Chinese Lord of Hell. 'We have her in our power.'

'I can enchant him; make him want to ride me to the clouds. Then drop him from a great height and kill him,' offered the Water Horse. 'That would be such fun, and he wouldn't be able to resist my beauty, no human can, not like someone else in this circle who it seems can.' She looked pointedly at Ma Mica, the other horse in the circle.

He ignored her.

'Not only do we have a problem with the boy, we also have a problem with the Guardians of Cardiff.' said the Enchanter, totally ignoring the offer.

'The Dragons . . . THE WELSH DRAGONS? You cannot be serious. Exactly when did they start to interfere in Chinese affairs?' snarled the Lord of Hell. 'They are not even Chinese Dragons, so why should they interfere with Chinese concerns?'

'The boy believes in the Jade Emperor!' The words Jade Emperor hung for what seemed like an eternity on the frosty air. To the wicked creatures gathered there at the stone circle it was a name so terrible that even they, shook in their shoes.

'We all know the trouble that causes. Those who that Jade Emperor has his eye on, those he protects, are difficult to deal with. Their souls belong to the Emperor . . . this girl is beloved by one such young man.'

The listening owl leaned slightly forward, bending his ear to hear more clearly.

'The point is, has she given her soul to . . . '

'No, the violin is buying her soul . . .' snapped the Enchanter. 'The spirits of the violin are persuading her. She is buying it with her obsession for it and music. Nothing else matters to the girl.'

'Before I was so rudely interrupted . . .' said Anku, glaring icily at the interrupter,

'I was going to ask, had she given her soul to the Jade

Emperor, does she know he loves people and does she return this boy's love?'

'She is totally unaware of both loves.'

'Ah . . . Then what we need to do, is to make sure we have her soul a lot quicker than we did the other girl's, whose blood went into the varnish.' Anku paused, measuring her words carefully. 'If we do not, the Jade Emperor will intervene and claim her back, and the violin will be destroyed. That would be the end to all our plans for world domination.'

'We have to have a plan to thwart the Jade Emperor and stop him from rescuing this girl and if we can take out half of Cardiff and those pesky Welsh Dragons as well, so much the better. Especially the Jade Emperor's son who disguises himself as the Great Green Dragon . . .' The Enchanter let out a sigh. 'But how?'

The debate raged fast and furious around the circle until finally it was decided to enlist the menace of the Cardiff streets, the Seagulls, to help them keep an eye on what was going on, not only in the lives of Xiao Mai and Jay Lee but also what was going on with the Guardians of the city. They were to bring every little bit of gossip, every scrap of damning paper from rubbish bins, to the Enchanter. They were to act as spies and messengers. When the time came all the members of the stone circle would be prepared to do their part if called upon to ensure that Xiao Mai paid the price for her obsession and the Jade Emperor was defeated for ever more.

Dawn started to streak the sky as the meeting broke up and the members of the stone circle faded into the rising ground-mist and the owl flew on silent wings to his favourite perch next to the Great Green Dragon on the dome of city hall.

Chapter 5

Busking

It was the following second Saturday that Xiao Mai laid the crocodile-skin violin case down on the pavement outside St John's Church, not far from the Owen Glendower public house and just opposite to the Bright House store. She sat down on the black crescent marble benches and waited for her friends to arrive. They were going to busk and try to raise money for Xiao Mai's living expenses. As she sat waiting for them, she did not notice the little Red Dragon hiding behind the church railings. Nor did she notice the tall thin man from the violin shop, minus his strange clothes and his hair not hanging loose about his face, but plaited in a neat pigtail like the ancient Chinese farmers, sitting outside the Pub opposite, in a stainless-steel chair, at a round stainless-steel table, sipping a cup of green tea. She did not notice his eyes dart to the violin case at her feet.

Her thoughts had wandered back to the previous two weeks; they had been such a source of delight to her.

Practice sessions had just flowed and she quite forgot time as the music poured forth from the violin and sometimes she forgot to eat but that didn't matter as she never felt hungry, she was losing weight but she didn't mind. Her violin lessons had all gone very well and he teachers were delighted with her progress.

'Amazing what a good instrument can do,' barked her Professor of Classical Music. He was a stickler for technique.

'Wonderful! Such expression! Such depth to your playing now Xiao Mai,' gushed Dr Julia Mazurka, the visiting lecturer from the Warsaw School of Music.

Then the conductor of the University orchestra, Dr Henry Purcell, happened to hear her playing in the practice rooms, poked his head around the door and exclaimed.

'Beautiful, Xiao Mai, your haunting rendering of Tchaikovsky's Dying Swan just captures the pathos of the piece and is utterly unforgettable . . . I can hardly stop the tears.'

'XieXie Laoshi, thank you, thank you teacher Purcell,' she had replied giving him a polite little Chinese bow.

'I would like you to play the solo when we perform at the Christmas concert at the Albert Hall,' he went on. 'Her Majesty the Queen and the President of the United States will be there. It might well launch your solo career.'

'Me Laoshi? But I am only a first-year student', she replied.

'Yes you, and do not be late for rehearsals. They are on a Thursday evening from six until eight in the main Music Hall. Oh, and before I forget, the whole of the University Orchestra will join with the Welsh Symphony Orchestra presenting a Summer Prom in the Castle grounds just before exams.'

With that, he had closed the door gently murmuring, 'such talent, such pathos, such an honour for me and for the University to have a student with such rare talent. This will really put the University on the map,' as he wandered down the corridor.

How Xiao Mai longed for fame and fortune. If she had that, then she could help her family, help her community to lead a better life. She knew that her father, a poor Gansu farmer, worked long hours in the fields to enable him to send her a hundred Yuan a month; to him it was a lot of money, in Wales it didn't last long. Her mother spent nearly all her spare time sewing beautiful embroidered insoles for rich people's shoes. Every month she would leave her cave village and clamber on board the local bus at six in the morning and travel the two-hour journey to the capital city of Gansu, Lanzhou, where she would sit with her basket on the ground in the main shopping area of Xiguan selling her wares. Sometimes she was moved on by police; sometimes her beautiful work was confiscated because she did not have a licence. Sometimes her goods would be kicked and scattered far and wide and the enforcement officers would laugh as she tried to gather up her wares into her broken baskets.

Xiao Mai saw her friends turn the corner by the Santander Building Society shop and waved to them. Jay Lee had his cello strapped to his back, Can Ding his double bass and Apple, (she didn't like using her Chinese name), carried her viola.

Soon they were ready to start. At Xiao Mai's signal they all lifted their bows and started to play a lovely Strauss waltz.

Everyone stopped shopping, everyone stopped rushing around, conversations ceased. Coffee cups were put back on tables. Arguments ceased, smiles replaced frowns. Men bowed to the ladies, boys bowed to girls. First one person, then another, then another started dancing. Men swept unknown women into their arms, women danced with women. Some danced alone, but not for long, partner changed partner, boy danced with girl. Even those who were handicapped and in wheelchairs danced, whirling their chairs around to the music.

The students laughed with joy. Their music had made the normally staid citizens of Cardiff dance in the streets, just like the citizens of their own Chinese home towns danced in all the open spaces they could find.

The tempo changed to a quick-step and then a fox-trot, then from fox-trot to line-dance music. The people danced on. It was as if they were enchanted, partners changed, patterns changed. The people were smiling, laughing, singing along to country and western songs and even songs from musicals.

One by one the musicians stopped playing, until only Xiao Mai was left making the music . . . she did not stop stomping and playing, roars of appreciation rose from the dancing crowd. Xiao Mai, flushed with excitement, was totally under the control of the violin.

'Faster! Faster Xiao Mai! Oh what fun!' sang the violin. 'Such a long time since I played dance music.' The little diamonds on the pegs seemed to glitter and giggle.

'She is becoming far too obsessed with that instrument,' observed Jay Lee, 'sometimes I wish we had never ever set eyes on it.'

'You are right, she is obsessed with it,' replied Apple,

'she didn't go to bed until four this morning. I heard her coming in and asked her where she had been. She said in Roath Park, down by the lake, playing the violin.'

'That time in the morning? She should have been in bed asleep.'

'That's not all. She said that as she was playing she saw a seal swimming and diving, dancing in the moonlit waters of the lake. It seemed as if they both were somehow involved in a performance for the Great Green Dragon sitting at the base of the little lighthouse.'

'But Xiao Mai is a good communist, she doesn't believe in the powers of Dragons, nor does she believe in anything supernatural.'

'But she says she saw them.'

'Hallucinated you mean.' Can Ding laughed.

Apples glared at him.

'Then she realised it was late when the town clock struck three. By that time a policeman on patrol spotted her standing there in the moonlight and told her to go home to bed.'

'A seal in the lake? You must be joking!' exclaimed Jay Lee.

'There is a statue of Billy the seal in Victoria Park, but she died years ago! Her skeleton is in the museum, so she is as dead as dead can be. Not unless her bones magically grew flesh and she flip-flopped herself all the way to Roath Park' joked Can Ding. 'And a Green Dragon, now I have heard everything! Xiao Mai must be seeing things or else she is going quite mad.'

'I am seriously worried about her,' said Jay Lee gloomily.

'Why, because she has found a new love...the Violin?'

'No! It is all the other stuff that has started to happen.

She never spends time with us anymore, never seems to joke and laugh, never wants to go out. She spends time down by the lake or the river playing that dratted instrument.'

'She's not eating either, see how thin she has become,' remarked Apple.

'She can't keep it up not sleeping and not eating, she will be really ill if she is not careful,' observed Can Ding, leaning on his double bass.

All three stared gloomily at their friend, what was the matter with her? Ever since she had acquired the violin she had done nothing but play it. Day and night she practiced, forgetting to eat and forgetting to sleep. She was getting paler and thinner by the day.

'If she goes on like this she will die of exhaustion, both mental and physical. This obsession with the violin and perfection just has to stop,' Jay Lee stated angrily. 'I want to smash it into little pieces.'

Xiao Mai stopped playing and bowed to the dancers. Money rained into the crocodile-skin case. When it was full, it snapped shut like a live creature of the deep, snapping its jaws upon a victim.

'Encore! Encore! Encore!' the crowd yelled.

Xiao Mai smiled and pushed back her blue black hair from her forehead. Once again she lifted the violin and raised the bow.

'No! No! No!' Screeched the Little Dragon, but his voice was not heard. 'You will die Xiao Mai! You will die of exhaustion.'

She did not hear him. 'She will die . . .' His little voice, like a whisper, travelled like a Dandelion seed-head on the wind towards the old clock tower of the Castle.

The thin old man rubbed his bony hands together in satisfaction, the enchantment was working; soon there would be another soul lost to the violin. Better still, the citizens of Cardiff were also under the spell, and soon they would be able to be manipulated like puppets on a string. *But where had that warning voice come from?* His piercing gaze picked out Jay Lee and he decided that somehow Jay Lee would have to be disposed of. His influence was far too great on Xiao Mai. Then there was the problem of the Dragon Guardians and the Jade Emperor. The world was no longer The Jade Emperor's to command, it was his, the Enchanter's, world now. He could manipulate people. Once they gave over their free will to him they never ever got it back.

At that moment a giant seagull flew down onto the Enchanter's table and grabbed a chip from his plate.

'What is your will, Oh master?' it squawked, almost choking on the heat of the chip.

'You are out of order doing what you have just done.' scolded the Enchanter. 'Filthy dirty bird! How disgusting, stealing food from people's plates like that. No wonder you are twice the size of ordinary seagulls. Time your tribe learned to eat fish from the sea like you were meant to, not human food! It is disgusting the way your seagull gangs maraud the streets, tearing open rubbish bags and strewing the contents all over the streets.'

'Then we wouldn't be useful to you, Oh Master' squawked the seagull calmly. 'If we did what we were supposed to do, you wouldn't get the information you need to carry out your evil plans against the citizens of Cardiff.'

'True, true, quite true,' agreed the Enchanter, nodding

his head slightly. 'But next time do not steal my chips. I don't want your dirty beak anywhere near my food. Do you understand?'

The sea gull bobbed its head down towards the plate of chips. The Enchanter banged his fist down on the table.

'No! Leave my chips alone.'

The seagull lowered its head in a mock kowtow bow.

'I have something to tell you master.'

'What is it, squawk it out.'

'Xiao Mai saw Billy the seal and the Great Green Dragon General last night in Roath Park!'

'Did she speak to them? Was anyone else with her, like those Chinese students over there?' his bony finger stabbed in the direction of the students.

'Don't think so.'

'See that Chinese boy over there?' The seagull twisted his head round to look in the direction the bony finger was pointing. 'I want you to stalk and harass him, dive-bomb him, splat him, peck him, steal his chips, and disturb his conversations . . . whatever you have to do to make his life a misery here in Cardiff do it . . . and bring me information about him. Damming information you understand?'

'What about that Cat?' squawked the seagull pointing his left wing in the direction of the Bengal Tiger cat that sat sunning itself at Jay Lee's feet.

'Kill it . . . tear out its eyes . . . stab it . . . bite off its claws one by one, cut its tail in little pieces, tear its fur out, do whatever you have to do, but get rid of it.' ordered the Enchanter. 'Or *ignore* it, after all it is only a cat.'

'But it is his Guardian,' cried the seagull, spreading his wings and flying to the highest vantage point on St John's church. 'It is his Guardian.'

The Enchanter shook his fist at the bird, then quietly drew his finger across his throat. The seagull understood.

Just as Xiao Mai's bow was about to come down on the strings in a wild gypsy dance, the bell in the Clock Tower of City Hall, started to boom. It boomed three times . . . then a half-boom. Slowly, solemnly the booms rang out over the city. Everything stopped as if held in time. The cars, the buses, the dancers, the Big Issue seller, and Xiao Mai poised with bow in mid-air ready to bring it down upon the strings of the enchanted violin. All as still as statues not moving and not breathing.

'What on Earth!' exclaimed the small Dragon, as he looked towards the Castle clock and understanding dawned as the mediaeval knight, Keeper of the Castle, waved his steel clad hand.

Chapter 6

Castell Coch

That first autumn term passed swiftly, until it seemed as if they had been in Cardiff forever. One bright December day Jay Lee managed to persuade Xiao Mai to leave her practising and the violin behind, to go on a visit to Castell Goch.

'You need some exercise and fresh air,' he declared.

'Jay Lee, I must practice otherwise I will never make the grade and my family will have sacrificed everything for me for nothing.'

'Look my dear little friend, (Xiao Paniol), just take a break will you and come and enjoy some exercise and do some sightseeing. Why you haven't been in Cardiff Castle yet, nor have you done Tony Lloyd's famous guided tour of Cardiff. Ever since you got that instrument from the old man you haven't been much fun at all. Practice! Practice! Practice! That is all you do now. P...R...A...C...T...I...C...E. Just come and have some fun. P...L...E...A...S...E?'

Xiao Mai looked at him, loosened the bow and tucked

the violin lovingly into its crocodile-skin case, which shut with a snap like teeth closing on teeth.

'OK,' she sighed 'I am coming. Where are we going?'

'On a cycle ride along the Taff to Castell Coch.'

'I don't have a bike.'

'You do now; I borrowed Apple's for you. Come on no excuses. '

Mounting the bicycles, they joined the river Taff path in Bute Park and cycled beside the river, crossing the bouncing white suspension bridge, and stopping to feed the horses in the nearby field grass.   On and on their wheels rolled, spokes sparkling in the autumn sunshine, until they came to the beech woods at the very edge of the city. Continuing on the muddy leaf-strewn path, they came to the place where the Taff plunged through a gorge. Above them, on what seemed like a rocky platform, towered the fairy tale Red Castle. Castell Goch, her fairy-tale coned towers just peeping out of the canopy of the beech wood that grew up the mountain side.

'How beautiful,' sighed Xiao Mai letting out a breath and tucking her blue-black hair behind her ears. 'Just like a fairy castle.'

They climbed up through the woods, wheeling the bikes up the steep path until they came to the front of the Castle; they crossed the drawbridge and entered the great gates, where the jagged teeth of the portcullis hung above their heads, and into the small round courtyard, with its red wooden gallery. There they left their bicycles chained up to the admissions hut.   In high spirits they went off to explore the Castle, with its three towers. Inside one they found a beautiful drawing room with colourful-hand painted pictures of Aesop's fables on the walls. But they did not notice that one of the paintings contained a cat, a Bengal Tiger cat, nor did they notice that the cat seemed to move from painting to painting as they moved about the Castle. Nor did they notice the little Red Dragon door-stop that held open doors for them as they passed through each door into the room beyond. And they definitely did not notice that one of the figures on the chimney-piece of the beautiful fireplace, depicting the three fates - infancy, adulthood and old-age - looked remarkably like the old man from the violin shop. He was busy cutting the thread of life that the other two figures held. A closer look, had they noticed, would have revealed that the faces of the other two fates resembled them, Jay Lee and Xiao Mai. But they did not recognise the likenesses, they were too busy looking at the wonderful blue and gold-domed ceiling and marvelling at the decorative butterflies, intricate in their delicate beauty. The two Guardians, however, recognised the message of the fireplace and followed their charges very closely throughout the tour, making sure that they were only a whisker away from them, just in case the evil Enchanter decided to pounce on Xiao Mai and end her life.

He, however, had other motives for being at Castell Coch. He waited until the pair made their way to the downstairs tea room and were sitting drinking cups of English Earl Grey tea, and eating slices of homemade Victoria sandwich. Then he started weaving spells. Spells to capture Xiao Mai's thoughts and tip her into a quarrel with Jay Lee.

'Have you enjoyed the trip Xiao Mai?' Jay lee asked.

'Yes very much. But I need to get back and practice the

violin. I am not ready for my lesson tomorrow.'

Jay Lee could not help himself. His voice held a note of irritation.

'Xiao Mai I just wish you were not so obsessive about that instrument, it is ruining your life.'

'So you keep saying Jay, what's the matter . . . are you jealous or something? That's it, isn't it? You are jealous. Fancy being jealous of a musical instrument.'

The tiny figure of the Enchanter hidden within the painting on the wall of the café rubbed his tiny hands in glee and tucked them into the copious sleeves of his blue and white Jalapa. His plan was working, the spells were working, and the mother of all quarrels was about to break out and the relationship between these two would be broken. Xiao Mai's soul would be his forever.

'The violin is evil Xiao Mai. It talks, and violins do not talk if they are real violins.'

Xiao Mai glared at him.

'So,' she hissed, 'what are you trying to tell me?'

'Get rid of it Xiao Mai, get rid of your obsessions, become normal again.'

'How, pray, am I to practise without the violin?' Her hands were shaking with rage, she was prepared to defend her beloved violin like a tigress defends her cubs.

'The Jade Emperor can help you . . . '

'The who?' she asked incredulously wondering if her ears were playing tricks on her.

'The Jade Emperor, you know, the King of Heaven,'

She drew her breath in sharply, and as she exhaled her words dropped like icicles into the frosty atmosphere.

'Listen Jay Lee, the Jade Emperor is a figment of your imagination, like the Dragon Guardians. Have you ever seen the Jade Emperor?'

'Well no, but I have seen pictures of him, what people think he might be like.'

'Where exactly did you see those pictures?'

'On the internet.'

'Precisely. On the internet. I bet it was on Wikipedia as well.'

Jay Lee rushed on regardless, not heeding the warning signs.

'Okay, then it is like this. In order for the Jade Emperor to help, you must first of all believe that he exists and you must have faith that he will hear your requests and answer them.'

Xiao Mai was furious and her words spat out of her mouth like an angry cat.

'Have faith? We Chinese are taught from baby-hood that to have a faith or any kind of belief system other than the communist party is wrong. Or have you forgotten, Jay Lee? We need to believe in ourselves and in the great communist movement.'

'Ah, but that is where you are wrong . . . '

He was on dangerous ground now.

She held up her hand.

'Look Jay Lee Woo, I am not having this conversation with you. DO you UNDERSTAND? There is no such person as the Jade Emperor, no such beings as Guardians and certainly no such being as the Green Dragon General or Red Dragon General. They are statues Jay Lee. Do you hear me? Statues that your vivid imagination has given life to. It is time you stopped this nonsense about faith, Dragons, Jade Emperors and the like and got back to reality, the reality of communism.' She rose from the table, donned her cycling helmet and stalked out of the café, leaving Jay Lee to pay the bill.

Furiously she pedalled towards Cardiff, anger driving her legs as she flew along the Taff path. The Little Dragon, a very worried expression in his little golden eyes, bounced up and down on the luggage carrier behind her, but she was completely unaware of his presence. Coming to the end of the Taff path, she pedalled through Bute Park towards the main gate nearly knocking down a child on a scooter.

'Watch where you are going . . . Learn the Highway Code before you take to the streets,' yelled his angry mother after the retreating cyclist.

Xiao Mai threw the bike in the backyard of number 12 Fanny Street and stormed into the house and through to her room, which was at the top of a steep flight of stairs. Grabbing the violin, she flew out of the door and ran nearly all the way to the music practice rooms.

She had had enough of Jay Lee going on and on about the Jade Emperor and having faith and asking for his help. She was a good communist. *Hadn't the good Chairman Mao, in the old days after the revolution, declared that all faith was a figment of the imagination? Hadn't he ordered that all temples and churches be destroyed and all books burned that contained any reference to any form of faith?* A little voice surfaced in her mind. *'Yes, but Grandmother believed in the Jade Emperor, she kept the stories in her heart, stories that when written down had been burnt. But Grandma had told her the stories in secret. Now under the new regime these stories were being told more openly. There might be some grain of truth in them after all, especially if they had survived generations.'*

She had calmed down by the time she reached her practice room. Opening the battered case, she lovingly lifted out the precious instrument. The little lights on the pegs twinkled and sparkled as she tightened up the strings, tuning the instrument to perfect pitch. Then she tucked the chin-piece beneath her chin, lifted the bow and started to play. But instead of playing beautiful music the instrument started to sing words.

'I am your love. I am your passion, I am your husband, your lover, your boyfriend, your friend. I am your mother and your father . . . I am your child. I am all the loves you will ever need Xiao Mai, I am all the loves you will ever need. Play me Xiao Mai. I am your heart's desire, I am everything to you . . . I am your all. Play me . . . '

Xiao Mai played and played, one piece after another, and the beautiful music crept out from beneath the door of the practice room and into the silent building. The small figure of the wicked Enchanter hiding behind the red fire extinguisher in the corridor, smiled his thin-lipped smile and once again rubbed his hands in satisfaction at all the mischief he had caused. *His plan was working; the girl was completely obsessed with the violin. It was everything to her: boyfriend, husband, father, baby, Yes, especially baby. She looked after the instrument as if it were a new-born child. He had her in his grip, or nearly . . . if only she wouldn't wear the colours of the welsh flag or have that pesky little mascot of a Red Dragon that always seemed to be there with her. What was it the seagull had said he was? A Guardian? Yes a Guardian that was it. Whilst she was surrounded by Dragons he could not touch her . . . finish her off.* He frowned a tiny frown that creased his forehead. He would have to get rid of the Guardian somehow. *Perhaps burning him; or throwing him into the Taff would be a good way. But then if he threw him into the Taff he would float out to sea and there was a strong possibility that he might end up back on shore, one could never tell with the tides around the Bristol Channel… or he could chop him up into tiny little pieces, sliver by sliver, before he threw him in the Taff…? No burning the little pest was a far better idea.*

Chapter 7

Jay Lee meets the Green Dragon.

Christmas came and went and so did Chinese New Year, then Easter. Xiao Mai grew increasingly thin and pale, and devoted herself more and more to the violin. Sometimes she would play in a concert in London, to great acclaim. But no evil befell her outside of Cardiff. Always Jay Lee and the Guardians went with her.

Once a month she would busk outside St John's church and every month the Enchanter would sit at his table outside the pub and watch her and the dancing crowds. And every time the great seagull would report to the evil Enchanter, bringing some titbits of information he and the seagull gangs had gleaned from the ravaging of the bins, stealing food and bullying the residents of the city.

The Guardians always made sure that they were on duty that day, calling in reinforcements, so that the Enchanter could not act to claim her soul. But they all knew it was only a matter of time before he did. Spring passed into summer and with it came news of a great concert to be held in the grounds of the Castle.

Jay Lee was very worried about Xiao Mai, instead of rejoicing in her success at the London Concert and the invitation from the President of the United States to go to Washington to play for him at the White House. She had become more obsessed than ever with the violin, going out at all hours to play in the open spaces of Cardiff. She seemed to enjoy playing in the moonlight down by the lake or river. Wherever she played she would see the apparition of Billy the seal dancing in the water to the music she made. The little Red Dragon was her constant companion. He would half walk, half fly to keep up with her, then would hide himself not far from the crocodile-skin case in order to protect her if he could from the wiles of the Crocodile Guardian of the violin who, occasionally, when touched by the magic of the music, would assume his original shape and take a dip in the water. Whenever that happened Billy would jump onto the base of the lighthouse and honk loudly in alarm. The Clock would strike an unusual hour and Xiao Mai would be restored to her right mind again.

One night, at about eleven, Xiao Mai let herself out of her shared student house in Fanny Street and walked quickly towards Roath Park hugging the violin case to her. She did not notice that she was being followed by Jay Lee, who kept a good distance back. Every time she stopped, he stopped, flattening himself against walls and hiding in alleyways until he heard her footsteps once again. Following Jay Lee on stealthy paws was his Guardian, the Bengal Tiger cat.

Eventually Xiao Mai reached Roath Park and climbed over the railings. Jay Lee waited until she had settled down to playing the violin and was oblivious to all else, then he followed. Just as he reached the top of the wrought-iron gates the giant seagull dive-bombed him, almost knocking him off. A great splat of seagull poo landed in his hair. The bird wheeled and came in again, flying low, Jay Lee in his sights. The cat snarled and leapt for the gull, catching a mouthful of tail feathers. With a squawk of indignation the seagull flew off and nursed his injured pride in a tall tree overlooking the place where Xiao Mai was playing.

Jay Lee jumped down from the gate and hid himself in the shadows, where he could watch Xiao Mai. The cat settled down in a nearby bed of leaves watching . . . waiting . . . his tail twitching and his ears pricked, listening. They saw Billy dancing . . . *'no harm there'* thought the cat, *'just a harmless little ghost. Who loves showing off.'*

Then they saw it . . . the metamorphosis of the violin case into a huge Crocodile. They saw him slip off the bank of the lake and into the water with hardly a splash; they saw him head straight for Billy. They saw the shape of the huge Green Dragon place itself between Billy and the Crocodile. They saw the Crocodile open its great mouth as if to do battle . . . They saw the fire shoot from the Dragon's mouth; they heard a loud voice which seemed to come from the Dragon.

'My time is not yet . . . it is not time for the final battle, belly-creeper. When it is, all of Cardiff will know about it. Return to where you came from.'

The Crocodile backed off, snarling, jaws snapping, afraid, back to the violin case. The watching seagull spy let out a tiny squawk of fear as he caught sight of the larger-than-life Green Dragon General flicking fire out of his mouth, his green wings raised, his front claws extended as far as they would go. Reaching for the Crocodile.

The Great Clock rang out the odd hour and Xiao Mai stopped playing, put the violin away and started to walk towards the gate. Billy waved a flipper and then faded into nothingness. As the Little Red Dragon passed the cat he transferred some thoughts. *'See what danger we are in?'*

'I saw,' thought replied the cat *'Scary stuff. It's a wonder that the Croc didn't kill Xiao Mai there and then.'*

'That's what he wants to do. He wants to drag her into the water and drown her by rolling over and over with her and not allowing her to breathe . . . but he can't whilst I and Billy are guarding her. Sometimes the Great Green Dragon or one of the other Dragons come to help me, because I am only a tiny Dragon and Billy is only a gentle little ghost. Xiao Mai must be kept safe.'

'Good Job the Dragon General was here tonight.'

The thoughts flew back and forth between the two animals.

'The Dragon General wants to see you and Jay Lee. When Xiao Mai has gone, he will meet you by the lighthouse . . . Oh, and before I forget, you need to deal with that seagull, he is a spy . . . before he deals with you.'

The cat waved a paw *'Zaijian worda paniol.'* In English, 'goodbye, my friend.'

'Show off!' muttered the Dragon, as he half ran, half flew after Xiao Mai.

Xiao Mai climbed over the gate and headed towards the Heath Hospital. The Little Red Dragon scuttling along at her heals. On her way past the cemetery her path was barred by the Evil Magician.

'You played well tonight Xiao Mai. But who was it I saw with you?' he smiled a tight-lipped smile and his eyes flashed fire and ice.

'No-one,'

'No-one? Come, come, my dear girl, you are not telling me the truth are you? You were playing for that young man and the Great Green Dragon and Billy the seal,'

'I was playing for myself and the violin.'

The Enchanter's eyes glowed red in the dark, his appearance began to change rapidly from old, to a young man, then old, then young again. His face changed rapidly from smiling, to evil, to anger. He stepped towards her, ready to strike her with his wand.

The crocodile-case changed into a large Crocodile that started to snap its jaws and move towards her.

'HELP!' she screamed, 'Won't somebody help me, please. Please, Jade Emperor, if you are real HELP me.'

At the mention of the Jade Emperor's name, the Crocodile returned to his case-shape, the Evil Enchanter faded from sight, and Xiao Mai saw she was facing a Christmas tree.

Mentally she shook herself; she had been scared of a tree. How silly.

Then she seemed to hear a voice a voice that came from a nearby life-size angel on a tombstone. There was a beautiful green light all around the angel, the voice from the light spoke directly into her mind.

'I wish you would trust me enough to let things happen naturally. I wish you would stop trying to control and predict what will happen. I guess that is a result of being brought up

without a belief system, without a belief in the Jade Emperor and in . . . '

'Stop right there.' Xiao Mai spoke the words out loud. 'I am self-sufficient, angel, or are you pretending to be the Jade Emperor who doesn't exist? You are not real. You are a white marble statue, either you are both a figment of my imagination or . . .' she took a breath, 'you only exist in stories. Everyone knows stories are made up.' She paused for breath then continued. 'I do not need your help. I know what I have to do to get to the top of my profession. I do not need your help or anyone else's help.'

The Little Dragon Guardian put his claws over his little pointy ears; he did not want to hear what Xiao Mai was saying to the green light. He was pretty sure it was the Jade Emperor masquerading as the stone angel.

'Child, child.' The voice was not audible to the human ear, only Xiao Mai knew what was being said. *'Child, if only you would relax and enjoy being with me. My love for you is everlasting. It will never ever die. I want to be your friend and your close companion. I have unconditional love for you . . . If only you would trust me.'*

'No, you are a figment of my imagination, nothing more. I need to trust in myself and my own capabilities. There is no such person as the Jade Emperor.'

'But I came when you called my name. I rescued you from the Enchanter.'

'GO AWAY Jade light! STOP talking stone angel,' she ordered. 'YOU DO NOT EXIST! You . . . do . . . not exist.' And she put her hands over her ears and looked away from the Jade light.

'As you wish, Xiao Mai, as you wish. But remember this, my love for you is everlasting, unconditional love. I am here

for you. Remember, joy is the invention of the Jade Emperor. You need joy, Xiao Mai, you need joy in your life. We will meet again when you call on my name. . .cry out for me when your life is in the greatest danger. You will remember our conversation and believe.'

'No I won't' she replied defiantly, as the green light faded and the angel returned to white marble.

The cat gazed at Jay Lee with amber eyes, 'Come let's go and meet the Great Dragon, son of the Jade Emperor,' he said, for once successfully transferring his thought to Jay Lee's mind. Jay Lee rose stiffly to his feet. The cat set off towards the lighthouse, his tail straight up in the air like the umbrella of a tour guide. Jay Lee followed.

'Welcome Jay Lee, son of China, follower of my father the Jade Emperor,' said the Dragon in sonorous tones.

'How do you know my name?' stuttered Jay Lee.

'Bow, bow, before the Prince, the mighty Dragon, son of the Jade Emperor,' hissed the cat.

Jay Lee bowed from the waist.

'I know your heart Jay Lee. I know that you love Xiao Mai.'

'Yes Sir, I do with all my heart.'

'Do not indulge yourself in self-pity or rage Jay Lee; that will get you nowhere.'

The words hung in the silence between them.

'I know that you are worried about Xiao Mai and rightly so. It is as it should be. But you are a follower of the Jade Emperor and she is not . . . Is that right?'

'Yes Sir. She knows nothing, except what I have tried to tell her about the Jade Emperor.'

'I see, you did well to tell her, Jay Lee, about my father, I mean. But you failed to protect her when she first met the Enchanter. You failed to stop her playing that instrument even though deep in your heart you knew that it was evil.'

'Yes Sir, I am sorry, Sir. I would give my life for Xiao Mai, Sir.'

'I know you would Jay Lee, but this battle has to be fought in the realm of the supernatural, pure power against evil power. You know the ancient Chinese symbol of the ying and the yang? '

Jay Lee nodded.

'We are fighting a battle unseen by mankind, a battle for a soul. This takes place in another dimension, in a world hidden, as if by a voile curtain, from the world of men; the division is so thin, like gossamer silk. Those who look can see this other world. To them it is a reality, but to the rest it simply does not exist because they do not want to see it.'

Jay Lee sighed a deep, sad sigh and a tear started to trickle down his left cheek.

'Come to me, come to me, my son, my friend. Put your hand in my claw, open up to me, rage at me. I can take all your anger and let it drop off my scales . . . but others more vulnerable cannot take it . . . they do not understand what you are going through.'

'Green Dragon, Master . . . I always feel deep peace when I see you. Now the anger and hurt are going.'

The Dragon laughed.

'I am peace, that is my name in the Kingdom of the Jade Emperor, I am known as the Prince that brings peace.'

Jay lee looked deep into the Dragon's golden eyes; a deep peace filled his whole body. Then he snuggled down between the Dragon's wing and leg. The great Green Dragon covered him with his wing, like a mother hen covers her chicks, and said softly,

'Come my son from the land of Dragons, come and tell me everything; all your worries, all your cares and your problems, because talking to me will enable you to see things from a different angle. As you open up to me my thoughts will flow into your mind and my song will lodge itself in your heart, and my love will surround you like a blanket.'

How long he lay there, talking to the Great Dragon, Jay Lee did not know, He felt warmth, comfort, a clearing of his mind. He had sobbed his heart out to the Great Dragon. The Dragon had held him closer and by his very being, poured love and comfort into Jay Lee's suffering soul.

After what seemed a life-time of pure comfort and security, the Great Dragon turned his head, looked at Jay Lee with his great golden eyes full of love, and said softly,

'I will fight this battle for you and rescue your girlfriend. But you must promise me that you will stay close to your Guardian, the cat, and that you will look after Xiao Mai for ever, once I have released her from the power of the Enchanter.'

'I promise, Sir.'

'Good. Now climb on my back and I will fly you back to your house in Mary Street.' He chuckled a deep, throaty chuckle 'Funny how you students love those streets named after teachers who taught at the local school.'

Jay Lee and the cat scrambled up onto the back of the Dragon and he took off into the night sky.

Chapter 8

Concert in the Castle.

The audience shuffled with expectation, spotlights lit up the orchestra as they tuned up. Then the audience broke into polite applause as the conductor, resplendent in black-tailed suit with a Dragon-flag waistcoat and red bow-tie walked onto the podium, bowed to the audience, turned, bowed to the orchestra, tapped his baton on the side of the music stand and waited. The orchestra jumped to action, bows poised, brass and wind instruments lifted to lips, drum-sticks raised. The Conductor lifted his white baton. A hush descended on the audience gathered within the Castle grounds. The baton waved faster as notes of 'In the Hall of the Mountain King,' part of the Peer Gynt suite by Grieg stole onto the evening air.

Slowly, silently, menacingly, the terrible Evil Ones that had gathered at the stone circle and their minions crept to their prearranged battle stations around the perimeter of the inner Castle wall. Nobody noticed the terrible Evil ones take their place in strategic locations. Their allies, the seagulls, gathered on the battlements, but nobody noticed. Nobody noticed the Guardians of the wall and the Dragon Guardians of Cardiff gather on the outer walls of the Castle and mark each Evil One, ready to pounce should they make a move, waiting, watching for the Evil Enchanter to make his move and more important still, to see what the Green Dragon General would do. But nobody noticed. Silently, the waiting Dragons and stone creatures and statues from around the city took note of the enemy's positions, watching and waiting for the Enchanter to make his move on Xiao Mai's life. The piece came to its dramatic end, the audience burst into deafening applause. The conductor bowed, the orchestra shuffled. Then snapped to performance mode.

The conductor brought his baton down and the orchestra burst into Mussorgsky's 'Night on the Bare Mountain'. The music carried the audience away to the distant mountain and in their minds pictures flashed of a sinister mountain where witches gathered to dance wildly and cast spells around a fairy tale castle with cone-shaped turrets that peeped through the trees and guarded to the road to Caerphilly and the valleys. The audience was enraptured and broke into thunderous applause as the music came to a tumultuous and dramatic end.

They gasped as they saw a Jade spotlight swing upwards to the topmost parapet of the Great Keep of Cardiff Castle, where a slender figure stood, bow in hand, her white dress fluttering in the cool evening breeze. The light turned to purest white. The Conductor lifted his white baton and sweet soft music of Beethoven's Violin Concerto in D major op 61, stole onto the evening air. Xiao Mai bowed slightly forwards, living the music, letting it enter the fibres of her body; her very soul. The light shone on the white music scores on the metal stands of the orchestra. Xiao Mai shifted the bow slightly, testing its tension, lifted the violin to her shoulder and then, using the upper register of the violin, started to play.

'What fun!' sang the violin, 'Together we make great music Xiao Mai; together we sing like angels.'

Xiao Mai's long fingers flew over the finger-board.

The French horns took up the refrain that sounded like a march. Xiao Mai paused, lowered her bow and glanced to one side. She lifted her face to the heavens and closed her eyes. Then started to play once more . . .

Nobody noticed the large Kingfisher-like bird settle on the parapet behind Xiao Mai.

Imperceptibly, the bird grew larger and still larger. Until his silhouette dwarfed the slender figure. Suddenly, his great beak made a furious stabbing movement. Xiao Mai staggered, lost her balance . . . and fell.

'Jade Emperor save me, I don't want to die . . .' she screamed as she fell.

The bird swooped and caught the flying instrument in his great beak. The audience gasped in horror as Xiao Mai's limp body tumbled down the walls of the Castle in slow motion. It seemed to hang there, falling, for ever.

Time elongated as the whole tragic scene took place in slow motion before their eyes. Suddenly a bright Jade light enveloped the audience and orchestra. They sat, frozen in time, unable to move . . . silent witnesses of the drama.

All around them, within the great courtyard of the Castle, in hand-to-hand, hand-to-claw, claw-to-claw, teeth-to-teeth combat, the battle raged between the Evil Ones and the Guardians of the city. Like arrows, the seagulls hurtled towards the Guardians, whirling, diving, and pecking. One by one they fell, crumpled little mounds of feathers beneath the tramping feet of the Guardian Warriors doing battle, determined to rid the city of the Evil Ones forever. All this time Xiao Mai was in suspended falling mode.

There was a sound of rushing wings as the Red Dragon General swooped low in a ground-plummeting nosedive; he arched underneath the falling girl and caught her on his broad back. Banking steeply, he swooped over the Castle curtain wall, over the canal and into Bute Park. He landed near the standing stones, stark and dark in the moonlight. Gently he shook the unconscious girl from his back onto the soft, springy grass. There was a tiny plonk as the Little Dragon Guardian landed on the grass beside the still and crumpled figure. Tears streaming down his little red snout and twisting his little red paws in sorrow.

'Is she dead?' he asked fearfully.

'No not dead, but in a coma.' came the reply. 'Come, little friend, and help me lay her on the altar-stone. There she must rest until the Great Green Dragon General has . . .' his voice trembled ever so slightly . . . 'vanquished the Evil Enchanter and broken the violin.'

Tenderly they laid her frail, emaciated body on the great altar-stone in the middle of the stone circle, arranged her long floating white dress and tidied her long, dark hair. The Little Dragon brought flowers and strewed them over the sleeping girl. Then the great Red Dragon took the laurel circlet from off his right leg and gently placed it around Xiao Mai's head. It fitted perfectly.

'Sleep and get well, Xiao Mai, sleep and get well.'

As the wreath of red laurel leaves settled around Xiao Mai's forehead, a shaft of pure Jade light beamed from the highest heaven and struck the unconscious girl in the heart.

A warm Jade light spread throughout her body restoring her emaciated limbs to roundness, her skin to smoothness like cream, and her hair to the lustre of a pure black pearl. Her dress of purest white danced with the colours of the rainbow. The crown of laurel leaves glowed red.

The silence was broken.

'This is my daughter.' The words were solemn, the voice indescribable in its deep beauty and resonance.

'Her soul has been bought at a great price. An innocent is prepared to die for her. At this moment he is about to give his life's blood. His innocent blood claims her back from the Evil Enchanter for me' . . . the voice faltered, a slight tremble could be heard . . . 'My son's innocent blood claims her back from a life of obsession and starvation. She will not die . . . her soul will not be imprisoned in the violin of obsession and disorder. She is mine.'

The beam of pure Jade light shifted to the girl's forehead and touched the crown of red laurel leaves.

'This is the crown of Victory.'

The voice took on a triumphant note.

'Victory over obsession.'

'My daughter is FREE.'

The voice paused, then spoke again into the great silence that surrounded the stone circle. The watching trees listened, their leaves rustling ever so slightly in the warm summer breeze.

'She will wake to a new life when the battle is over and the victory is won. From this time her name will no longer be Xiao Mai, but Lily. Pure, innocent, Lily, as pure as the newly-fallen snow. From now on her whole life will be one of pure fragrance and beauty. From this day she becomes my beloved daughter. From this day she will be known as

Princess Lily the precious and beloved daughter of the Jade Emperor.'

The Jade light faded. Princess Lily lay quietly sleeping on the great stone altar.

'Adopted daughter? When did the Jade Emperor adopt Xiao Mai?' whispered the Little Dragon.

'As from now,' replied the Red Dragon in sonorous tones. 'As from now, my Little Dragon, you are the Guardian of a Princess of Heaven.'

The Little Dragon's eyes grew round with surprise and his little chest puffed out with his new-found importance.

'I will? But what about the Evil Enchanter?'

'The Great Green Dragon General will defeat him; even now the battle is raging over the Castle, for supremacy. It will result in the death of the Great Dragon General but the Evil Enchanter will be vanquished!'

'But why and how can this happen, if the Dragon General dies?'

'In order for Xiao Mai to be rescued from a life of tortuous existence, and at her death become one of the voices of the violin, the General has to fight the Enchanter and give his life to break the spell created in the mists of time, which the Enchanter put on the violin at its completion.'

'Why does he have to be the one?' asked the Little Dragon, combing Xiao Mai's hair with his claws.

'Because he does it willingly and he has never ever done any wrong whatsoever, his heart is pure.'

The Great Red Dragon bowed to the sleeping figure on the flat stone.

'Sleep, Princess Lily.'

'No, you have it wrong, her name is Xiao Mai,' interrupted the Little Dragon.

'Remember, little friend, the Jade Emperor has just changed her name, or were you not listening?' replied the Red Dragon patiently.

The Little Dragon s eyebrow arched, but he bit his little red tongue and smiled sweetly at the Great Red Dragon General and did not say a word.

'I must go and reinforce the troops at the Castle. There will be a great battle tonight and victory will be ours. You stay and guard the Princess.' The Great Dragon spread his wings and rose into the air and over the Castle wall to join the battle.

The little Red Dragon settled down to watch over the sleeping princess.

'Who would have thought it,' he said softly to himself. 'Who would have thought that the Great Jade Emperor would adopt Xiao Mai and give her a new name, Princess Lily the pure . . . and I, the Little Dragon . . . I am her guardian.' He sighed a deep, deep, sigh of pure satisfaction.

Chapter 9

The Great Battle

The audience gasped in horror as they saw a huge, green Dragon spotlighted on the ramparts of the turret. Then, as the gigantic Kookaburra-like, bird rose in the air, the audience held their breath and watched in stunned silence as the two great creatures clashed furiously in claw-to-claw battle. The Dragon spat fire as the bird tried to gouge out his eyes, flying again and again at his head. The Dragon twisted and turned, slashed with his tail, raked with his claws.

After what seemed like hours, the giant bird broke loose, rose into the air, twisted, then swooped and plummeted towards his opponent like a diving spitfire in the Battle of Britain, rolling and catching him behind his head. The Dragon twisted and turned but could not break the hold of the strong beak. Then the giant bird landed on the topmost turret and started to beat his prey's long body against the grey walls of the Castle. The walls groaned and boomed as the body of the great Dragon hit them again and again, bones crunched under the impact, shattered and broke, but the giant bird did not release his grip or stop his actions until every bone in the great, green body was shattered and the writhing ceased.

The audience were aghast at what was taking place before their eyes. But could not move.

'Oh no,' gasped Jay Lee, a sob catching in his throat. 'The Dragon General is dead. Xiao Mai will never be free of the Enchanter now. He has won.'

The huge bird gripped the Dragon's limp body in his massive talons and flew above the flagpole. Letting out a mighty squawk, he let it drop onto the great spike. It pierced the Dragon's heart and water and blood gushed out, staining the Welsh Flag. Then the Enchanter bound the body to the pole with cords of spiders' silk. There the great limp body of the Great Green Dragon hung dripping blood and water until his lovely green scales turned a deathly white.

For the whole of the next day, and into the evening and on into the following night he hung there, a pitiful sight. The night faded into dawn and dawn into a blazing day. The flies gathered and buzzed around the broken body of the great Dragon Guardian. The Enchanter sat in his Kookaburra shape on the turret gloating, the violin at his feet. The day passed into sultry evening, an evening when the stars refused to shine and the moon hid herself in sorrow behind a cloud. It was dark, as dark as the darkness is in the bowels of the earth. Utter darkness, blackest darkness,

The stunned crowd waited, shell-shocked, watching, unmoving, sobbing. The great Clock struck twelve midnight, then thirteen. A bright light, pure Jade in colour, shone from the sky, pinpointing the broken body of the Dragon. The deep baritone voice of the Jade Emperor rang out.

'My son is dead. He died so that evil could be defeated and the power of the instrument of obsession broken. Innocent souls have died, but will be freed to come and live with me in my palace. My son will live again!'

A fork of Jade green lightning shot from the sky, green flames danced around the parapet touching both the body of the Dragon and the violin. There came a mighty crack, as the violin broke into a thousand pieces which fell into the moat like autumn leaves drifting on the wind. Slowly the wraiths of the lost girls captured in the violin drifted heavenwards. The lightning forked again, striking the Enchanter. Heaven's thunder-drums rolled as the great deceiver, the evil Enchanter, burst into flames and was slowly consumed by fire.

Seeing their leader was dead, gone forever, the remaining other Evils slunk off into the darkness, afraid of getting the same treatment.

Jay Lee, tears streaming down his cheeks, turned to leave the scene of carnage. His heart felt as if it would break in two. He had lost everything. His one true love, Xiao Mai, his will to live, but above all his heart grieved, felt like it had been dragged out of his body as he had witnessed his friend and mentor, the Great Green Dragon, battle with the evil Enchanter and die. He, Jay Lee, had caused this to happen by not stopping Xiao Mai from playing the violin. Now she was probably dead and the Great Dragon was dead, all because he had not accepted the responsibility for keeping Xiao Mai safe.

Another great crack like lightning forked down from

the Jade cloud. Jay Lee turned to gaze once more on the body of his friend. The long, broken body of the Green Dragon General began to glow . . . there was a hissing sound . . . a tearing, cracking sound, as the Great Green Dragon General burst his bonds, heaved his long body off the flagpole and flung himself joyfully into the air to meet his father, the Jade Emperor.

Jay Lee clasped his hands in joy. 'He is alive!' he screamed to the heavens, 'He is alive! The Great Green Dragon General has defeated the evil Enchanter. HE IS ALIVE!' Jay Lee began to dance.

'Stop that Jay Lee,' the cat Guardian spoke into his mind. 'Follow me, I will take you to Xiao Mai.'

Jay Lee followed the upright tail of the Bengal Tiger cat out through the gate and past the empty Animal Wall, through the gate by the Tea House and across the lawns to the great stone circle. There, on the altar-stone, in the middle of the great stone circle, he saw Xiao Mai sleeping. The laurel crown on her head glowing a deep, ruby red and her dress shimmering with rainbow colours. He looked down on the sleeping girl and bent over and brushed her lips gently with his. Her eyelids fluttered and she woke up.

'Come Xiao Mai, let's go home,'

'I am not called Xiao Mai any longer,' she smiled a beautiful smile.

Jay Lee raised an eyebrow.

'I am the daughter of the Jade Emperor, he rescued me, restored me, gave me a new life and a new name.'

'What is it?'

'Princess Lily the Pure,' chorused the Dragon and the cat.

'All right, Princess Lily the Pure,' said Jay Lee, getting down on one knee, 'will you marry me and come home with me to China?'

'I will,' she said simply, 'Oh, I will Jay Lee.'

'For a while I thought I had lost you, beloved Lily, I thought I had lost you forever to the Evil Enchanter and the violin.'

Princess Lily smiled, 'For a while we have lived simultaneously in two dimensions, Jay Lee. I know now that what I did was wrong and the Great Dragon General gave his life for me. We are both children of the Jade Emperor. Who knows what adventures he has in store for us in the future; but right now, I am content to go home with you to China.'

This is where my tale ends, a tale of obsession, love, sacrifice and new birth, a tale recorded forever in the deep, secret places of Cardiff.

A Note from the Author.

I hope you enjoy reading this tale of obsession. There are many processes to writing a story like this. First comes the idea, then comes the plan and the draft. Next comes the re reading and improving. Then onto at least two proof readers. After changes are made another proof reader proofs your book. It does however pay to be cautious and a final read by the author is essential before finally submitting it to be published. A long drawn out process. But even then in this modern age of technology, there can still be mistakes made that would not otherwise have been made by the type setters of old.

Often the computer does not agree with what you have written and argues with spelling and punctuation, you write British English and the computer tells you American English, or does not allow you to put an accent, where you know you need to have an accent or a sign peculiar to a specific language. For instance the Mandarin used in this book is pinion but I was unable to add the accents. So I apologise in advance for any tiny little mistakes you might find but remember all the people who participated in the production of this book are human and humans make mistakes.

Enjoy the read.
Carol Logan.

About the Author

Carol loves writing. That's pretty much it! This new book 'The Enchanted Violin,' along with The stories in 'Max the Incredible Cat' reflect her talent in writing and her sense of fun and enthusiasm for life.

Carol is a graduate of Reading and Brunel Universities, she has also completed Diplomas from Cardiff University and Newcastle College. Carol taught in Primary, middle and secondary schools before lecturing in British and American literature at Lanzhou University of Technology in China. She is published author of 'When Sea Billows Roll' a personal journey through cancer and 'Travellers Tales', short travel stories. She is also a published artist. Carol uploads weekly stories and chats on her Facebook page, 'Carol's Books and Story Time' (Look it up). Carol is the mother of four grown-up daughters and Granny to three granddaughters and two grandsons. She loves travelling and has many friends throughout the world including quite a following in China.

By Ken Jones

32394121R00045

Printed in Poland
by Amazon Fulfillment
Poland Sp. z o.o., Wrocław